THE CASE OF THE U.S. NAVY ADVENTURE™

A novelization by Deborah Perlberg

WILL SOLVE ANY CRIME • BY DINNER TIME ™

DUALSTAR PUBLICATIONS PARACHUTE PRESS

SCHOLASTIC INC.

New York   Toronto   London   Auckland   Sydney

DUALSTAR PUBLICATIONS   PARACHUTE PRESS

Dualstar Publications
c/o Thorne and Company
1801 Century Park East
Los Angeles, CA 90067

Parachute Press
156 Fifth Avenue
Suite 325
New York, NY 10010

Published by Scholastic Inc.

With special thanks to Robert Thorne and Harold Weitzberg.

Printed in the U.S.A.
November 1997
ISBN: 0-590-88015-2
A B C D E F G H I J

Ready for Adventure?

It was the best of times. It was the worst of times. Actually it was bedtime when our great-grandmother would read us stories of mystery and suspense. It was then that we decided to be detectives.

The story you are about to read is one of the cases from the files of the Olsen and Olsen Mystery Agency. We call it *The Case Of The United States Navy Adventure*.

UFOs? Flying saucers? Aliens right here on earth?

We didn't believe it, but the FOOFFOS— Friends Of Our Friends From Outer Space— asked us to investigate. Were there really aliens on earth? We had to learn the truth. And that's how we found out that the earth was in big danger. Someone had to save it!

Could we do it? We weren't worried. Because we always live up to our motto: Will Solve Any Crime By Dinner Time!

Rat-à-tat-atata! Ziiiiiip—ka-boom!

The noise of Laser Invaders echoed through the upstairs hall of our house. Laser Invaders was our brother Trent's brand new, hand-held video game. He hadn't stopped playing since he got it last week.

Beep-beep! Zap!

"Hooray!" Trent appeared in the bedroom I share with my twin sister, Ashley.

"Another alien bit the dust!" Trent cheered. "I just made it to level five!"

"Great. Now you can stop playing that game," I told him. "Video games are fun. But those noises are driving me totally crazy!"

"Me too!" Ashley added.

I'm Mary-Kate Olsen. Ashley and I are the

Trenchcoat Twins. We're detectives! We love solving mysteries.

And it was no mystery why Trent was bothering us. Trent is eleven, and he *loves* to drive us crazy. He can be a real pain.

Bleeep-bleep!

"Trent!" I yelled. "For the last time—stop playing that game!"

"Uh, Mary-Kate," Ashley said. "That noise isn't Laser Invaders. It's the phone ringing upstairs in our office."

Oooops!

Ashley and I raced out of our bedroom. We ran up the steps to our office in the attic. That's where we run the Olsen and Olsen Mystery Agency.

We burst into the attic.

I grabbed my blue phone. Ashley answered her pink phone.

"Hello! Olsen and Olsen Mystery Agency," I began. "Will solve any crime—"

"By dinner time," Ashley finished.

"Greetings, fellow earthlings," a voice replied. "This is Roberta."

"And Hank," a second voice said.

"And Alvin," a third voice added. "We're the FOOFFOS!"

"The whats?" I asked.

"FOOFFOS. That stands for Friends Of Our Friends From Outer Space," Roberta explained. "We're the friends of aliens! You know, creatures from other planets!"

"We've been searching the skies for years," Hank went on. "We look for UFOs."

"Wait—what are those?" I asked.

"UFO stands for unidentified flying object," Roberta explained. "Like a spaceship from Mars, Jupiter, or some other planet. Or anything else that flies—but we can't tell what it is!"

"We watch the sky every night for bright lights or strange flying things," Hank added.

"Of course, they usually turn out to be airplanes." Roberta sighed. She sounded very disappointed. I felt badly for her.

"Did you ever actually see a UFO?" I asked them.

"Not until last night," Hank said.

"And boy, did we hit the jackpot!" Roberta chuckled. "We spotted a whole flock of flying saucers! But that's not the best part."

"What's the best part?" Ashley asked.

"One of the flying saucers landed!" Hank exclaimed. "It crashed to the ground."

"It crashed? That sounds serious," I said. "Was anyone hurt?"

"We don't know. That's where you come in," Roberta replied. "We know the saucer crashed. But we don't know *where*."

"Right. We heard the crash. Then we saw some smoke. But we haven't been able to find the UFO," Hank explained. "You're detectives. *You* know how to find things— we need your help!"

"And after you find it, you can help us talk to the aliens," Roberta finished.

"Please help us," Alvin added. "Pretty please?"

"Let me get this straight," Ashley said. "You want us to find a crashed flying saucer—and talk to the aliens on board?"

"Exactly!" Roberta sighed happily.

"I'm not sure I *want* to talk to aliens," I said.

"Me either," Ashley agreed.

"Oh, don't be afraid," Roberta told us. "It could be very exciting! Just think, we'll learn all about other worlds."

"And life on other planets," Hank added.

"And how other life-forms think," Alvin said.

Hmmmmm.

"That *does* sound pretty interesting," I said.

"Great! When can you get here?" Roberta asked.

"Where is here?" I asked.

"We're on an island near Hawaii," Roberta

9

replied. "It's called the Edge-of-the-World. It's a deserted island."

"Actually, it's not *totally* deserted," Hank added. "After all, *we're* here!" He chuckled.

"You'll find us at the Edge-of-the-World Hotel," Roberta went on. "We're the only guests right now. That's how we like it. Too many people would scare the aliens away!"

"Well, we don't know much about flying saucers or aliens," I said. "But we'll be glad to help."

"Great!" Roberta exclaimed. "Look for us at the picnic area when you get to the Edge-of-the-World."

Ashley and I said good-bye. I pulled out my detective manual. Great-grandma Olive gave Ashley and me the manuals. She loves mysteries. She taught us how to be detectives.

"Let's look up the chapter on UFOs," I said. "Maybe it will tell us something about how to talk to aliens."

"I hate to say this, Mary-Kate," Ashley said. "But I just looked. And there isn't a chapter on UFOs—or aliens. I don't think we should take this case."

"Not take the case? You're kidding, right?" I asked.

Sometimes it's hard to believe we're twins.

We're both nine years old. We both have strawberry blond hair and blue eyes. We may look alike, but sometimes we don't act alike—or even think alike!

Ashley thinks and thinks about every problem. And then she thinks some more. Not me. I work on hunches. I always want to jump right in!

"I know!" I snapped my fingers. "Let's look up UFOs in Mom and Dad's computer library."

Ashley and I rushed downstairs to our parents' study.

Our mom and dad are computer experts. They know everything about computers—

and they taught us how to use them to find out anything we need to know.

"I'll look up flying saucers first," I said as we rushed into the study.

Beep! Zap! Blast!

"Oh, no!" I groaned. Trent was in the study, playing his hand-held video game, Laser Invaders!

Our dog, Clue, was hiding under the computer desk. Her paws covered her ears. She whined at the noise.

"Did you say flying saucers?" Trent made a face. "I guess you're working on another one of your dumb mysteries."

"Solving mysteries isn't dumb," I said. "It's useful. We help people. Playing Laser Invaders all day long is dumb!"

"For your information, Laser Invaders is not dumb. You have to be really smart to play it," Trent replied.

"Really? Why?" I asked.

"First, you have to figure out where the

moving targets will be," Trent said. "Then you have to figure out the exact angle you need to aim the laser beam. And *then* you have to figure out when to push the trigger button. It takes a calm hand, a steady eye, and nerves of steel."

"Sorry, Trent," I said. "I still don't see why you have to be smart to zap phony aliens."

"Oh, yeah?" Trent snapped.

"Yeah!" I snapped back.

"Oh, yeah?" Trent repeated.

"Yeah!" Ashley jumped in.

"Oh, yeah?"

Our six-year-old sister, Lizzie, ran into the study. "Yeah!" she shouted.

"You don't even know what we're talking about," Trent said. "Do you?"

Lizzie shook her head. "It doesn't matter. I agree with Mary-Kate and Ashley," she told him.

Ashley and I smiled. "See?" I said. "Even Lizzie knows it's a dumb game."

"It is *not* dumb!" Trent shouted.

"Will you kids cut it out?" Mom stuck her head into the study. Dad was right behind her. "You three have been arguing over that game all week! I can't take it anymore!"

"Trent started it," I said.

"They started it," Trent said at the same time.

Mom held up her hands for quiet. "I don't care who started it," she told us. "I just want it to stop."

"And I know exactly how to do it," Dad said. "This family needs a trip to a far-off, tropical island."

"Go on a trip? Now?" I turned to Ashley with a horrified look. "But we have a case to solve! We can't go anywhere!"

Chapter 2

"A family trip is exactly what we need," Dad said. "Spending quality time together will stop you kids from arguing."

"It will?" Trent asked.

"Dad said so, didn't he?" Ashley argued.

"Hold it!" Mom said. "Maybe your dad is right. And we were just offered a job in Hawaii."

Ashley and I exchanged surprised glances. Hawaii was close to the Edge-of-the-World — and the FOOFFOS!

"This job is at the U.S. Navy base at Pearl Harbor in Hawaii," Dad explained. "The Navy asked us to design a new computer training program."

"Right," Mom added. "But we can take

some time to go sightseeing too."

"That's why I already stopped by the travel agency," Dad said. "I picked up these vacation folders."

Dad showed us a whole pile of colorful folders. There were pictures of different hotels.

"Look," I whispered. I poked Ashley in the ribs. "There's a folder for the Edge-of-the-World Hotel!"

Ashley pulled it from the pile. She handed it to Mom. "I really, really like the way this place looks," she said.

"It's very pretty." Mom nodded. "It looks nice and private too. I'd like to stay someplace quiet when we're not busy working."

Mom and Dad quickly read through the folder. "This place sounds perfect," Dad agreed.

"Let's tell the Navy we'll take the job," Mom said.

"I'll order the airplane tickets," Dad said.

"I'll start packing!" Mom added.

"Can Clue come too?" Ashley asked.

"Of course," Mom answered.

Yes!

Ashley and I cheered.

We were on the case!

Three days later, we arrived at the Edge-of-the-World Hotel. It was nearly deserted. The hotel stood by itself. It was the only building on the whole island.

The hotel was very pretty. It sat on a huge beach right on the sparkling Pacific Ocean. Palm trees grew all around it. The rest of the island was covered with a wild tropical jungle. Everywhere we looked we saw bright jungle plants and flowers.

"Let's go meet the FOOFFOS," I whispered to Ashley.

"Uh, Mary-Kate and I have some exploring to do," Ashley told Mom and Dad. "See you later!"

"Wait a minute," Dad replied. "We saved

17

today to spend some quality time *together*!"

Ashley and I exchanged worried looks. We wanted to start work on our case!

Trent turned to Dad. "Wouldn't you and Mom like some quality time together first— just the two of you?" he asked.

"Well, that would be nice," Dad replied. "In fact, it's a great idea!" He turned to me. "Mary-Kate, I think it's your turn to watch Lizzie."

"Hurray!" Lizzie cheered.

Dad and Mom hurried off together for a swim. "See you kids at lunchtime," Mom called.

Yes!

"I have to admit, that was pretty quick thinking, Trent," I said. "Now we can investigate our UFO mystery. Thanks."

"You're welcome," Trent replied. "And thank you for watching Lizzie. Now I can I try for the tenth skill level on my video game."

"But we can't take Lizzie!" I said. "We have a mystery to solve!"

Lizzie thinks we're great detectives. She loves to follow us around. But sometimes she slows us down.

Tweeet! Zaaaaap! Ka-boom!

Trent zapped another alien invader. "I just reached the tenth level!" he exclaimed.

"Good for you! And I know you won't mind watching Lizzie while you try for the eleventh!" Ashley and I tried to hurry away.

"No way!" Trent shook his head. "Dad said it's your turn. Besides, I'm minding Clue."

Clue was already asleep under a bed. "Big deal," said Ashley.

"Okay, Trent," I said. "We'll give you our whole allowance for this week—if you take care of Lizzie."

"No!" Lizzie shouted. "I want to come with you."

"No, you don't," Ashley told her. "We're

going through bushes. There will be all sorts of stinging bugs."

"Big ones," I added. I took a tube of bug spray from my suitcase and put it in my backpack.

"Oh," Lizzie said. "You're right. I don't want to come."

"How about *two* weeks allowance?" Ashley asked Trent.

"It's a deal," Trent said with a big grin.

Ashley and I grabbed our rented purple bikes and matching purple helmets. We pedaled off to meet the FOOFFOS.

"Roberta said we'd find them near the picnic area," I told Ashley. We headed down the picnic path together. We rode through the jungle for almost ten minutes.

"Look!" Ashley pointed straight ahead.

I spotted three people waiting by the picnic tables. The tall woman with reddish-brown hair had to be Roberta. Her bright orange dress was as colorful as the tropical flowers. Roberta was busy aiming a telescope into the sky.

A man with short dark hair stood next to her. He wore bright blue plaid pants and a bright blue shirt. He was busy reading a map.

A second man stood nearby. He wore bright green pants and a matching flowered print shirt. He was scribbling notes on a pad of paper.

"Are you Roberta, Hank, and Alvin?" I called.

"Shhh!" Roberta waved for us to come closer. "Follow us—so we can talk without anyone hearing us," she whispered.

"But there isn't anyone around to hear us," Ashley pointed out.

"You can never be too careful where UFOs are concerned," Roberta said. She introduced everyone. Hank was the man in the flowered green shirt. Alvin wore the blue shirt.

I pulled out my detective notebook. "Tell me everything you know about the flock of flying saucers," I said.

"Well, we know that one flying saucer crashed into the jungle," Roberta said. "But other flying saucers pass overhead every ninety-three minutes."

"Exactly ninety-three minutes and ten seconds," Hank added.

"And they fly lower and lower every time we see them," Roberta said.

"I bet there's a real live alien inside each one of them!" Alvin exclaimed.

I wrote down everything they said.

"Where were you when the saucer crashed?" Ashley asked.

"Right here," Roberta answered. "We saw it fall somewhere on the other side of the island."

"But after it crashed, there was no trace of it," Hank added.

"Nope," Alvin said. "Only a big streak of

smoke over a clearing in the trees."

"Why don't you lead us to the clearing," I said. "That's probably where it landed."

"Wow! You are really clever detectives!" Roberta clapped me on the back.

Roberta, Hank, and Alvin led us through the jungle to the other side of the Edge-of-the-World.

"This is too, too exciting!" Roberta exclaimed.

"I can't believe we're really, finally, actually going to meet our first aliens!" Hank added.

"Yup," Alvin agreed.

The FOOFFOS stopped. Roberta pointed to a small clearing up ahead. "That's where we saw the smoke," she said.

We hurried into the clearing. The FOOF-FOS followed.

I was really excited. I couldn't believe we were about to see a real flying saucer!

"There it is! There's the spaceship!" Ashley

yelled. We raced together into the clearing.

I stopped short. "Is that the whole ship?" I asked. "It's awfully small."

The ship lay right-side up in the dirt. It was battered and smashed. It looked like a metal bowl about four feet across. The bowl was filled with metal tubes, tiny lights, and fancy-looking switches. Odd bits of wires and metal stuck out all over it.

"It looks more like a pile of junk than a real flying saucer," I said.

"There could still be aliens on board. Very small aliens," Ashley said. "Let's get closer."

"Come on, FOOFFOS," I called. "Let's take a closer look."

There was no answer. I turned around.

Alvin, Hank, and Roberta were trying to sneak away.

"Hey, where are you going?" Ashley called. "We thought you wanted to meet the aliens!"

"On second thought—we're too scared!"

Roberta answered. She turned and ran. Hank and Alvin disappeared into the jungle behind her.

I sighed. "Well, *I* still want to meet the aliens. Come on, Ashley." I grabbed her hand.

Ashley held on to my hand and squeezed it tightly. "I'm r-right behind you," she whispered.

We crept up to the saucer. Ashley leaned over it.

"Hello!" she called. "Are there any aliens in there?"

I held my breath as I waited for an answer.

"Earthlings, beware!" a weird voice rang out behind us. "You don't belong here! Leave now—and never return!"

Chapter 3

"An alien!" I exclaimed. "And he speaks really good English!"

"He sounds strange to me," Ashley replied. "Come on—let's get out of here!" She turned to leave.

I grabbed her arm. "We're not going anywhere," I told her. "We came to meet aliens, and we're going to meet them."

"But where are they?" Ashley asked. "That voice sounded like it came from the jungle."

"You're right," I said.

I gazed all around the clearing.

"Hello, aliens, wherever you are! We come in peace!" I yelled. "We're friendly earthlings!"

I heard snapping sounds, as if someone

were running away through the trees and bushes.

Then there was silence.

Hmmmmm.

Ashley and I searched the ground for footprints. We didn't find any.

"Do aliens even have footprints?" I asked.

Ashley shrugged. "How would I know?"

I sighed and pulled my notebook from my backpack. I wrote down our first clues. INFORMATION: Found crashed flying saucer. A strange voice warned us away. But no sight of aliens.

"There was something strange about that voice," I told Ashley. "Don't you wonder why it spoke English instead of some alien language?"

"Maybe the aliens studied English before they came here," Ashley replied.

"Maybe," I said. "But isn't it weird that we didn't see one of them?"

"Maybe they're hiding. Or maybe they're

invisible," Ashley said. "We don't know anything about them. But I do know that we should be very careful."

"True," I said. "But we also need to examine the evidence."

I pulled my magnifying glass and my hammer from my backpack.

I studied the inside and outside of the saucer. Then I tapped it with my hammer to see if it was solid.

Suddenly, steam hissed from the saucer. Sparks flew everywhere.

Klank! Tick! Fizz!

More sparks flew, and the whole ship started to shake and quiver.

Ka-boink!!

A metal panel sprang off the side of the ship. It flew into the air.

"Watch out!" I yelled.

The metal panel crashed to the ground.

We raced over to examine it. It was about two feet long and one foot wide.

"Look—there's some kind of writing on this panel," Ashley said.

We both studied the panel closely. The writing was made of letters formed by strange lines.

"I can't read this," I said. "It must be written in an alien language!"

"But there's something kind of familiar-looking about it," Ashley replied.

"Familiar?" I shrugged. "It looks totally weird to me."

"Let's check our laptop computers for clues," Ashley said.

We sat on two tree stumps and pulled our laptops from our backpacks.

I searched a file for information on alien languages. Ashley looked in the science file for information on UFOs.

Nothing.

"Maybe we're looking in the wrong places," I said. "But where *should* we look?"

"Beats me," Ashley replied. She checked

her watch. "It's almost time for lunch. We really have to go!"

"Okay," I said. "But we'd better take the panel with us, for evidence."

I picked up the panel and tucked it under my arm. "We can study this more later."

Ashley and I hurried back to our hotel room.

"I'll make a copy of the writing on this panel," I told Ashley. I pulled out my notebook and wrote. CLUE: Found alien writing on panel from space ship.

Then I made a copy of the strange-looking writing. I had just finished when the door to our room opened. Mom poked her head inside.

"There you are!" Mom said. "You're back just in time. We're all going out for lunch."

"Out where?" I asked. "I thought this island was deserted."

"It is," Mom replied. "That's why we're taking the ferry to the island of Oahu. The ferry is leaving right now. We have to hurry."

"But Mom, I need to write down stuff about this panel first," I told her. I showed her the panel.

"Bring it along, Mary-Kate. We're leaving right now," Mom said.

Mom, Dad, Trent, Ashley, Lizzie, Clue and I got on the ferry to Oahu.

"The water is so blue," Lizzie said. Ashley and I nodded. Everything was beautiful.

A short while later the ferry docked.

The island of Oahu was busy and bustling —and filled with hotels and restaurants.

"We can find anything we'd like to eat here," Dad said.

"Good! I want a hot dog," Lizzie said.

"Are you kidding? I can't wait to hit Honolulu Harry's Hamburgers," Trent said.

"No way!" I said. "Ashley and I want to try Spaghetti City!"

"Hamburgers," Trent said.

"Spaghetti!" I repeated.

"Stop arguing!" Mom exclaimed. "*I'll* pick the restaurant."

Ten minutes later we were seated around a big table in the Golden Dragon Hawaiian Chinese Restaurant. I slipped the panel under our table to keep it safe.

I picked up my menu. One side was printed in English. The other side was printed in Chinese.

"Ashley! Look at this!" I showed her the menu. "This writing is the same as the writing on our panel!"

Ashley's eyes opened wide in surprise. "You mean the writing on the panel is in Chinese?"

"I think so," I said.

I reached under the table and pulled the panel out. I showed it to Ashley.

"You're right! It is the same," Ashley said. "Does that mean the UFO is Chinese?"

"I guess so," I said.

"No wonder we couldn't find anything

about the saucer in our computers," Ashley said. "We *were* looking in the wrong places!"

"You're not kidding," I replied.

I pulled out my notebook. I crossed out my notes about the alien writing. Instead, I wrote: Found writing on panel—in Chinese.

"I'm really glad we figured out that the writing is Chinese," I said.

"I'm kind of glad this mystery has nothing to do with aliens from outer space," Ashley agreed.

"But there *is* a mystery about that saucer," I added. "And I have a hunch we're about to find out what it *really* is!"

"The first thing we need is more clues," I
told Ashley. I petted Clue. She was waiting
for us outside the restaurant where we had
just eaten lunch.

Mom and Dad were busy talking about
what to do next.

"I'd like to go sight-seeing," Mom said.

"Me, too!" Lizzie agreed.

"I want to find a video arcade," Trent put
in.

"Not me," Ashley said. "I'll go anyplace
but a video arcade."

"Oh, no," I groaned. "Here we go again!"

Mom frowned. "This vacation was sup-
posed to stop you kids from arguing. Let's
find a place we'll all enjoy. Someplace that's

fun for everyone." She turned to Dad. "Where would you suggest, Jack?"

"I'd like to tour the naval base at Pearl Harbor," Dad answered. "My old friend, Admiral Dewey, has invited the whole family over for a tour."

"Really?" Trent asked. "Could I get to see a real navy destroyer?"

"What's a navy destroyer?" Lizzie asked. "Some kind of video game?"

Trent laughed. "No, destroyers are great big ships," he explained. "They usually have a big cannon or guns on board. They are so cool!"

"Well, I just want to get a sailor hat to wear," Lizzie said. "Can I get one, Mom?"

"Sure!" Mom gave us all a big smile. "I'm just glad we finally found something everyone can enjoy."

"A tour doesn't sound like much fun to me," I complained.

"What do *you* think is fun?" Trent teased.

"Looking for UFOs?" He laughed loudly.

"What's all this about UFOs?" Mom asked. "Those other people staying at our hotel were talking about UFOs this morning."

"I remember that," Dad said. "The tall, red-haired woman was asking her two friends about flying saucers."

I nudged Ashley. "He means Roberta, Hank, and Alvin," I whispered.

"I guess it's because we're so near the naval base," Mom told him.

"What does the Navy have to do with UFOs?" I asked.

"The Navy is in charge of some very important space programs," Dad explained.

"I didn't know that!" I exchanged a look of surprise with Ashley.

"Would they know anything about Chinese spaceships?" Ashley asked.

"I suppose so," Mom answered.

"Then I change my mind! A tour does sound interesting to me," I said.

"Me too!" Ashley added. "Let's go see Admiral Dewey right now!"

"Yeah!" Lizzie added with a grin.

Dad's friend Admiral Dewey must have been *very* important. All the men and women sailors at the naval base knew we were there to see him—and they were *extra* nice to us.

First they showed us a ship docked in the water.

"That's a naval destroyer," Trent said. "Pretty amazing, huh?"

"It is pretty cool," I said.

Next the sailors let us tour a giant aircraft carrier.

"Aircraft carriers are like airports that float in the water," Trent told us.

"I can't believe how big it is," I said.

"I can't believe that a jet plane can land on a ship that's floating in the water!" Ashley exclaimed.

"That's because their decks are like long

runways," Trent explained. "The decks look about a gazillion feet long!" Trent was impressed. So were Ashley and I.

When our tour ended, the sailors brought us all genuine navy sailor hats to wear.

"I love my new hat!" Lizzie said.

Clue barked. She seemed to like the hat, too.

"Now it's time to meet Admiral Dewey." Dad nodded hello to a tall man with dark hair as he walked up to us.

Admiral Dewey looked very important. His uniform was very fancy. His shirt was decorated with lots of colorful stripes and medals above his pocket.

"I know you already had a special tour," the admiral said. "But is there anything else I can show you?"

Mom and Dad asked to see the computer room. I knew they could stay there for hours.

"Uh, Admiral Dewey—" I began. "Can

Ashley and I ask you some questions about spaceships?"

"That's my favorite thing to talk about!" The admiral beamed at Ashley and me. "Why don't you come into my office? That way I can find answers to your questions."

"Great!" I said. I grabbed Ashley's arm.

"Hey, wait! I'm coming too," Trent said.

"Uh, isn't it your job to watch Lizzie?" I asked.

Trent scowled at me. "But this is special," he said.

"I agree." Dad nodded to Trent. "Mom and I will watch Lizzie. You go with the admiral, Trent."

"All right!" Trent cheered. "Let's go, Admiral!"

Trent raced up ahead to walk with the admiral.

Ashley and I hurried behind them. Clue came with us.

"I hope Trent doesn't ask Admiral Dewey

any questions about Laser Invaders," I whispered to Ashley. She giggled.

As soon as we were inside Admiral Dewey's office, Ashley showed him the panel from the crashed flying saucer.

"Admiral, we were hoping you could tell us more about this," she began. "We think that it—"

"Grrrrr..."

Clue lowered her head and bared her teeth. She stared at the door.

"What is it, girl?" I asked. "What's wrong?"

Suddenly, we heard a familiar voice call out from the doorway behind us.

"What are you two doing here?"

I stared at Ashley in shock. "Th-that's the voice that warned us to stay away from the spaceship!"

We're Mary-Kate and Ashley—the Trenchcoat Twins. Our family was taking a vacation on an island near Hawaii. It was called the Edge-of-the-World.

That's where we met Alvin, Roberta, and Hank. They needed our help to solve a mystery. A flying saucer had landed somewhere on the island! Wow!

We found the flying saucer right away. But it looked like a pile of junk.

Ashley thought an alien might be trapped inside. "Hello?" she said to the pile of junk. "Are there any aliens in there?"

Suddenly we heard a voice. "Earthlings, beware!" it said. "Leave now—and never return!"

But we weren't afraid. We examined the flying saucer closely. I hit it with a hammer to see what it was made of.

Sparks flew from the flying saucer. And a metal panel shot into the air. The metal was covered with strange-looking writing. Could it be *alien* writing?

That afternoon, we visited a famous U.S. Navy base in Hawaii. The navy is in charge of some space programs. If anyone could help us with this mystery, they could!

We met Admiral Dewey. He said the navy was already on the case.

Oh, wow! This was a bigger mystery than we thought! And the panel we found was an important clue!

The admiral invited us onto his big navy ship.

It was so exciting working with the navy!

Another mystery solved! We were practically heroes—and the navy even gave us our very own uniforms! This was an out-of-this-world mystery. Did you figure it out?

Ashley grabbed me. I grabbed Ashley.

"Grrrrr…woof!" Clue leapt at the door.

I held my breath as I turned around.

A dark-haired man stood in the doorway.

The man looked amazed. "You!" he exclaimed. "What are you doing here?"

"You're the one who told us to get away from the crashed spaceship," I said. "What are *you* doing *here*?" We stared at each other in confusion.

"Do you all know each other?" Admiral Dewey asked.

The man turned to Admiral Dewey. "Why, these are the twins I told you about, sir. I saw them while I was working at the Edge-of-the-World."

"You were working there?" Ashley asked.

"Well, yes," the man replied. "I wanted to study the spaceship. And I didn't want anyone to ruin my research."

"What kind of research?" I asked.

"I study spaceships and rumors about UFOs," the man explained. "My name is Elmer Trombley," he added.

I stared at Mr. Trombley. "You mean you're a regular human being?"

"Of course he is." Admiral Dewey looked confused. "Mr. Trombley likes to come along when the Navy is doing an investigation."

"Do you mean that the Navy is already investigating the spaceship we found?" Ashley asked.

"Of course," the admiral replied. "We keep track of everything in the sky.

"Maybe we can all help each other," the admiral said. He turned to Ashley and me. "Tell us everything you found out so far."

Quickly, Ashley and I explained all about

the FOOFFOS and the crashed flying saucer.

"Wait a minute," Trent said. He stared at Ashley and me in surprise. "You guys found a spaceship on the island? A *real* spaceship?"

"That's right," the admiral answered. "I should have known the Trenchcoat Twins would already know all about my mystery."

"What mystery?" I asked.

"That 'flying saucer' is really a part of a satellite," Mr. Trombley answered. "A Chinese communications satellite."

"We use that satellite," the admiral explained. "Satellites can help send television and news broadcasts. Or they might help gather information about the weather. We need them to send information from one country to another all around the globe."

"Are there ever any people on board the satellites?" I asked.

"Or aliens?" Ashley added.

"No," the admiral answered with a smile. "There are no aliens on board. Why, there's no one on board at all!"

I wrote down the information in my notebook. INFORMATION: No life-forms on flying saucer.

Ooooops.

I erased "flying saucer" and wrote "satellite" instead.

"The FOOFFOS will be so disappointed," Ashley said. "No aliens at all."

"Someone should tell them right away," I said.

"I agree." The admiral dialed the Edge-of-the-World Hotel. A moment later, he was speaking to Roberta. He explained that the Navy was taking care of the piece of broken satellite. And that it wasn't a UFO. And that there were no aliens on the island.

Admiral Dewey hung up the phone. He smiled. "The FOOFFOS are going home to Ohio. They sounded glad there weren't any real aliens around," he told us.

"But if there weren't any aliens on board,

why did Mr. Trombley warn us away from the ship?" I asked.

The admiral smiled. "We don't want anyone to harm the satellite. So we have to be careful."

"It's already broken," I pointed out.

"Yes. But even when a satellite is down, it can still give us important information," the admiral replied. "Our petty officers went to the Edge-of-the-World right after you left. They brought the broken satellite here so we can study it."

"Oh!" Ashley nodded. "I guess you can use it to learn about all those *other* satellites."

"Other satellites?" The admiral frowned in confusion.

"Oh, no!" Mr. Trombley's eyes widened in alarm. "But—there shouldn't be any other satellites!"

Chapter 6

We told the admiral and Mr. Trombley what the FOOFFOS said about a flock of satellites—and how a new one flew overhead every ninety-three minutes.

"Roberta said they were getting lower every time," I added.

The admiral frowned. "There isn't any flock of satellites," he said. "There's just *one* satellite."

"Huh?" I said.

"What the FOOFFOS saw was just one satellite circling the earth," Mr. Trombley explained. "A satellite always has a set path. We call that an orbit."

"This satellite was in a low-level orbit," the admiral said. "That means it was flying in a circle around the earth, very close to the ground."

"I think I understand," I said. Ashley nodded.

"This satellite's orbit was low and fast. So it flew overhead about every ninety-three minutes," the admiral added. "Your 'flying saucer' was only one small piece that broke off that satellite."

"Wow. Isn't a broken satellite a big problem?" I asked.

"Yeah, isn't it?" Trent repeated.

"Not at all!" Mr. Trombley shook his head. "All satellites fall apart at some time."

"They do wear out," the admiral said. "And they're programmed to come apart over the ocean or some deserted place."

"Like the Edge-of-the-World?" I asked.

"Exactly." Admiral Dewey nodded. "But this piece fell off sooner than it should have. We've been helping the Chinese by tracking the satellite. We knew right away that it dropped out of its usual orbit."

"And if its orbit around the earth takes ninety-three minutes and twelve seconds—" Mr. Trombley went on.

"You mean ten seconds," Ashley said.

"What?" Mr. Trombley looked surprised.

"The FOOFFOS said the flock of satellites—I mean, the *one* satellite—was passing overhead every ninety-three minutes and *ten* seconds," Ashley repeated.

Mr. Trombley gasped. "B-but I thought it was twelve seconds!" He turned to Admiral Dewey. "Do you know what this means?"

"Of course I do." The admiral frowned. "It means everyone on earth is in danger!"

Chapter 7

"Excuse me, Admiral," I said. "But I don't understand. What difference does ten seconds or twelve seconds make?"

Trent groaned. "Even I know that!" he said. "That means that the satellite is moving much faster than it should be."

"This is terrible!" Mr. Trombley groaned. "There's been a mistake. A very *big* mistake!"

"I still don't get it," I said.

Mr. Trombley turned to me. "You just proved that my information about the satellite's orbit was wrong. It's moving faster than I thought. And that means that the satellite might not crash in a deserted area."

He pulled out a handkerchief and mopped sweat off his forehead. "If it falls on a big city, hundreds of people could get hurt!"

"Then somebody has to do something to stop it," I said.

"And fast," Ashley added.

"You're exactly right," the admiral replied.

"Shouldn't we warn everyone?" Ashley asked.

"We've already taken care of that," Admiral Dewey answered. "And we have a plan in place to solve the problem."

The admiral turned to a nearby sailor. "Petty Officer Richardson, call Captain Jones!" he ordered.

"Aye, aye, sir!" The sailor picked up a phone. "This is Petty Officer Richardson at Navy Base Pearl Harbor. Call for Captain Jones from Admiral Dewey," he said. He listened for a reply. "Captain Jones is standing by," he reported to the admiral.

"But what can Captain Jones do?" I asked.

"He can help bring our destroyer to the

right place on the ocean," the admiral explained. "We'll wait until the satellite flies overhead. Then we can shoot it down so it will land in the water."

"I see. Then all the people on earth will be safe," I said.

"Right. That's why I wasn't worried." The admiral checked his watch. "It's time to board the destroyer."

"Great! Let's go!" Trent shouted.

"This is so exciting," I said. Ashley, Clue, and I headed for the doorway.

A hand reached out and grabbed my arm.

"Hold it! I don't think *you're* going!"

Chapter 8

Mr. Trombley looked worried. "Kids and dogs don't belong on a navy destroyer!"

Admiral Dewey shook his head. "It's my decision, Mr. Trombley. This is official navy business."

"That's right!" I said.

"Woof!" Clue added.

The admiral smiled. "And I say these kids are special. So is their dog! I want them all to come along."

"Let's go, everyone," I called.

Clue ran ahead of us out of the admiral's office.

We quickly followed the admiral and Mr. Trombley across the pier. Then we headed up the gangplank. The gangplank is the walkway that leads up to a ship.

"This is one great destroyer," Trent whispered as we boarded the ship.

We saw three men already waiting on deck. The admiral pointed out Captain Jones, the Officer of the Deck, and the Petty Officer of the Watch. They looked so important!

Admiral Dewey climbed on board. He turned and saluted the flag at the rear of the ship. Then the Officer of the Deck, the Petty Officer, and Captain Jones all snapped him a salute.

Admiral Dewey saluted the captain in return. "Good afternoon, Captain Jones," he greeted him.

"Welcome aboard, sir," Captain Jones replied.

"Glad to be here. It seems we have a lot of work to do," the admiral told him. "What's going on?"

"It's worse than we thought, sir." Captain Jones took a deep breath. "You'd better come with me!"

Chapter 9

"Hurry!" Captain Jones said.

The captain led us down a narrow metal ladder to the deck right below the bridge.

"This is so cool!" Trent exclaimed.

"What is this place?" I asked.

"This is the Combat Information Center," the admiral told us. "The brains of the ship."

Everywhere we looked we saw huge maps of the world.

Computers filled the countertops.

Three large radar screens hung above the computers.

Ziiiiip—ka-boom!

Bleep-bleep! Zap!

The radar screens made sounds just like Laser Invaders! It was amazing.

"This is totally incredible," Trent said.

"We're ready to figure out the exact location of the satellite's new orbit," Captain Jones told the admiral.

"Are you ready to aim your secret weapon?" the admiral asked.

"Secret weapon? What is it?" Trent interrupted.

"They can't tell you," Mr. Trombley said. "It's a secret!"

"Sure we can tell him!" The admiral smiled at Trent. "The Navy has a new super-secret laser beam," he explained. "We can use it to bring down the satellite over the ocean. That way, it won't fall on anyone on earth."

"Wow. Amazing!" Trent exclaimed.

Ashley and I agreed.

Captain Jones turned to the petty officer who was checking the main radar screen. The screen was blank.

"When we find the satellite, it will show up as a small green dot on the radar screen,"

Captain Jones explained.

"No sight of the satellite yet, Captain," the petty officer reported. "I'll let you know as soon as I spot it."

Captain Jones glanced at his watch. "It's time for me to get up on the bridge," he said to the petty officer. "I'll wait for your directions. Then I'll steer this ship to the target point."

"That's the place where you need to wait for the satellite, right?" Trent asked. "That's where you'll use the new super-secret laser beam."

"That's right." The captain nodded at the petty officer. "Petty Officer Peters, call Lieutenant Bernson, the TAO."

"That's short for tactical action officer," the admiral told us. "Lieutenant Bernson is specially trained. He's the one who actually requests permission to fire the laser."

"Cool!" Trent's eyes widened in excitement. "I wish I could do that."

Captain Jones hurried up to the bridge. The bridge is one of the highest places on a ship. The captain steers the ship from the bridge.

A tall, blond-haired man stepped quickly into the command center. "Lieutenant Bernson reporting for duty, sir!"

The lieutenant stepped up to a set of controls. It was covered with buttons and knobs.

"Look at all those buttons!" Trent exclaimed. His hand brushed against a control knob.

"Oh, no!" Mr. Trombley groaned. "Now what have you done?"

Chapter 10

"What did I do?" Trent asked. He looked worried.

"You moved the button that aims the laser, that's what!" Mr. Trombley shouted. "Now it will miss the target!"

"Calm down," the admiral told Mr. Trombley. "Trent didn't move the laser."

"He didn't?" Mr. Trombley asked.

"He didn't even touch it," Lieutenant Bernson replied. "No harm done," he added.

"You'd better learn to relax," the admiral told Mr. Trombley. "Don't worry so much."

"Yes, sir," Mr. Trombley mumbled.

"The TAO will aim the laser at the satellite," the admiral told us. "Then he'll press that bright red button and fire."

"Just like Laser Invaders," Trent said.

"What's that?" Mr. Trombley asked.

"That's the name of Trent's new video game," I replied.

"And the secret weapon in Laser Invaders looks exactly like your secret laser weapon," Trent added.

"I doubt that!" Mr. Trombley laughed. "No kid's game is like this weapon."

Trent looked insulted. "It's a very scientific game," he said. "When you hit the final target, you move up a skill level. But you only get a chance for one shot at each level."

"And we'll probably get just one shot too," Admiral Dewey told him.

"We've found the satellite!" The petty officer in front of the main radar screen pointed to a small green dot.

"It will be over the target point in exactly seven minutes," he said.

It was all very exciting.

Ziiiiiip—ka-boom!

Bleep-bleep! Zap!

The room was suddenly so noisy that I could hardly hear anyone speaking. The computers were beeping and clapping. The green dot raced across the radar screen.

"There's the satellite!" The TAO picked up his telephone. "Captain, this is the TAO," he said. "We have a visual sighting of the satellite. Request permission to track and target satellite."

"That means he wants the captain's okay to follow the satellite with the laser beam," Admiral Dewey explained.

"Permission granted!" the captain answered.

"Aye, aye, sir!" the TAO replied.

We watched the green light blip across the radar screen.

Bleep-bleep! Zap!

"Sir, we have a good track on the satellite. We're locked and ready to fire," the TAO told the captain.

"They've aimed the laser at the satellite," Admiral Dewey explained.

"Stand by and fire on my order," the captain answered.

"Aye, aye, sir," the TAO said.

The TAO raised his finger above the red trigger button. The radar screen suddenly went crazy. Lots of green dots flashed all over it.

"I hear the radar going crazy," we heard the captain say over the phone. "Hold your fire!"

Mr. Trombley turned pale. "Oh, no!" he exclaimed. "Something must be terribly wrong!"

Chapter 11

"The radar is really going crazy!" Mr. Trombley stared in amazement. Now hundreds of green lights raced across the radar screens.

"What is it? What's wrong?" We heard Captain Jones yell into the phone.

"I've never seen anything like it!" Lieutenant Bernson muttered.

"Rrrrfff!" Clue barked. She ran over to Trent and leapt up at him.

Everyone turned to stare.

Trent frowned. "What? What did I do?" he asked. He held out his hands. He was grasping his video game.

"Oh, no!" Ashley smacked her hand against her forehead. "Not Laser Invaders!

You're the one causing the problem!"

"How could you play that game at a time like this?" I asked.

"I wasn't playing," Trent said. "I turned the game off."

"You *thought* you turned it off." I pointed to the game's tiny screen. It glowed. "That game was on."

"Let me see that game," Admiral Dewey demanded.

"Here it is, sir." Trent showed the video game to the admiral. He gave him a sheepish grin.

Admiral Dewey looked closely at the game. "I suppose this might be the problem. But it could be something else."

"Of course it's the problem!" Mr. Trombley said. His voice trembled nervously. "All those bleeping, zapping sounds must have mixed up the radar!"

He groaned. "Now we missed our chance to fire at the satellite—and all because of a silly, kids' video game!"

"I didn't mean to do it." Trent's voice was weak. His face turned pale. Sweat ran down his forehead. "I'm really, really sorry!"

"Sorry won't save this mission!" Mr. Trombley pulled at his hair. He looked ill.

"Now the satellite will crash for sure! Hundreds of people will get hurt! And there's nothing we can do to stop it!"

Trent looked so miserable I actually felt sorry for him.

"Hold on," the admiral told us. "Trent didn't cause the problem."

"He didn't?" Mr. Trombley was confused.

"No," Admiral Dewey replied. "An aircraft came along and confused the radar. But don't worry—this mission isn't in danger."

"It isn't?" Ashley asked.

"Not at all." Admiral Dewey answered. "I told you—the Navy is always prepared. Isn't that so, Lieutenant Bernson?"

The TAO smiled. "Sure. I can figure out where the satellite will be in another few minutes," he explained. "Then I'll have a second chance to get my shot."

"Cheer up, Trombley." The admiral clapped him on the back.

The admiral turned to the TAO. "Have you found the new target, Lieutenant?"

"Yes, sir! We have a track on the satellite," the TAO said. He called the captain to request permission to fire.

"You may fire when ready, Lieutenant Bernson," we heard the captain say.

The TAO again raised his finger above the red trigger button. "Stand by to fire," he said.

His finger dropped closer to the red button.

Admiral Dewey picked up the phone. He spoke quickly to Captain Jones.

"Hold it, Lieutenant!" the admiral said. "Whatever you do, don't fire yet!"

Chapter 13

"Don't fire?" Lieutenant Bernson asked in surprise.

"What's wrong now?" Mr. Trombley asked.

"Nothing," Admiral Dewey replied. He turned to Trent.

"But I hear you're an expert at Laser Invaders," the admiral said. "Why don't you nod your head when you think the operator should fire?"

"All right!" Trent grinned. He stood next to Lieutenant Bernson.

"Target approaching, sir," Lieutenant Bernson reported.

"Now watch the radar screens," the admiral told us. "You'll see the green dot get bigger as the satellite comes closer overhead."

We crowded around the screen. The green dot grew larger.

"Ready," the TAO called. "And…now!"

Trent nodded at the exact same time.

Ka-BOOOOOOM!!

The green dot on the radar screen grew brighter. Then it disappeared.

"Target destroyed!" the TAO said.

Ashley and I slapped Trent a high five.

So did the TAO, Admiral Dewey—and even Mr. Trombley!

Clue jumped up and licked Trent's face.

"I can't believe it," I murmured. "Trent *is* a good shot! He knew exactly when to fire the laser."

"If Trent were a TAO, he could have saved the world," Ashley added. "He could have been a real hero."

"You're all heroes to me," the admiral said.

Chapter 14

Admiral Dewey saluted Ashley, Trent, and me. "Thanks for helping us complete our mission," he said.

"You're welcome, Admiral Dewey," I replied.

"I hope this adventure will add to your research, Mr. Trombley," the admiral said.

"It should." Mr. Trombley beamed. He turned to Ashley and me. "You twins caught my mistake about the orbit's extra two seconds. And you realized that the 'flying saucer' was really a Chinese spaceship."

"You mean satellite," Ashley corrected him.

Mr. Trombley laughed. "Right," he said. "I meant to say 'satellite.'"

"And we figured out something else really

important," I pointed out.

"What's that?" the admiral asked.

"We figured out how to get away from Mom, Dad, and Lizzie," I joked.

"Uh-oh!" Ashley exclaimed.

"What's wrong?" I asked.

"We broke a family rule! We left the naval base—and we never told Mom and Dad where we were going!" Ashley looked worried.

"You're right!" I groaned. "We're in big trouble now!"

"Don't worry. I'll take care of it," Admiral Dewey told us.

The admiral called our parents and explained everything that had happened. They agreed to meet us when the ship docked back in Pearl Harbor.

As we left the ship we stopped to salute Captain Jones and Admiral Dewey.

"Request permission to depart," we said.

"Permission granted," Captain Jones

replied. He gave us a big smile.

We saluted the flag. Mom and Dad looked really surprised when we marched down the gangplank in our official, kid-sized navy uniforms.

Trent, Ashley, and I saluted Mom and Dad.

"Request permission to be forgiven for breaking the rules," I said.

Mom and Dad smiled. "Permission granted," Mom said. Lizzie giggled.

Mom glanced at her watch. "You're back pretty early," she told us. "You cracked this case way before dinner time."

"Then let's go out for an early dinner," Dad said. "What do you kids want to eat?"

"Fried chicken," I said.

"Chinese food!" Ashley said.

"No, barbecue!" Trent said.

I sighed. Here we go again!

Heroes or not, I guess some things never change!

Hi — from both of us!

The Trenchcoat Twins talking to space aliens? *Uh-oh!* We were really glad when the U.S. Navy stepped in. And we got to help them solve a problem that was really out-of-this-world! We couldn't wait to get back home. We needed a rest after so much excitement!

But we didn't get a rest. Instead we got a very strange phone call — inviting us to solve a super-spooky mystery!

You'll be haunted by the strange clues we found. Want to know how we cracked this ghostly case? Read all about it in *The Case Of Thorn Mansion.* In the meantime, if you have any questions, you can write us at:

MARY-KATE + ASHLEY'S FUN CLUB
859 HOLLYWOOD WAY, SUITE 412
BURBANK, CA 91505

We would love to hear from you!

*Love
Mary-Kate and Ashley*

The Adventures of
MARY-KATE & ASHLEY™

"MEET YOUR FAVORITE STARS" SWEEPSTAKES

Win a trip to meet Mary-Kate & Ashley Olsen on the set of their next production!

Complete this entry form and send to:
The Adventures of Mary-Kate & Ashley™
"Meet Your Favorite Stars" Sweepstakes
c/o Scholastic Trade Marketing Dept.
P.O. Box 7500
Jefferson City, MO 65102-7500

MARY-KATE & ASHLEY
"MEET YOUR FAVORITE STARS" SWEEPSTAKES

(please print)

Name_____

Address_____ State_____ Zip_____

City_____

Phone Number (_____)_____

Age_____

PARACHUTE

DUALSTAR
PUBLICATION

The Adventures of Mary-Kate & Ashley™ "Meet Your Favorite Stars" Sweepstakes

OFFICIAL RULES:

1. No purchase necessary.

2. To enter, complete the official entry form or hand print your name, address, and phone number along with the words "The Adventures of Mary-Kate & Ashley™ "Meet Your Favorite Stars" Sweepstakes" on a 3 x 5 card and mail to: The Adventures of Mary-Kate & Ashley™ "Meet Your Favorite Stars" Sweepstakes, c/o Scholastic Trade Marketing Dept., P.O. Box 7500, Jefferson City, MO 65102-7500, postmarked no later than February 28, 1998. Enter as often as you wish, but each entry must be mailed separately. One entry per envelope. Partially completed, illegible or mechanically reproduced entries will not be accepted. Sponsors are not responsible for lost, late, mutilated, illegible, stolen, postage-due, incomplete or misdirected entries. All entries become the property of Scholastic Inc. and will not be returned.

3. Sweepstakes open to all legal residents of the United States, who are between the ages of five and twelve by February 28, 1998 excluding employees and immediate family members of Scholastic Inc., Parachute Properties, Parachute Press and Parachute Publishing, L.L.C. and its respective subsidiaries and affiliates, officers, directors, shareholders, employees, agents, attorneys and other representatives (individually and collectively, "Parachute"), Warner Vision Entertainment, Dualstar Entertainment Group, Inc. and its subsidiaries and affiliates, officers, directors, shareholders, employees, agents, attorneys and other representatives (individually and collectively "Dualstar"), and their respective parent companies, affiliates, subsidiaries, advertising, promotion and fulfillment agencies, and the persons with whom each of the above are domiciled. Offer void where prohibited or restricted.

4. Odds of winning depend on total number of entries received. All prizes will be awarded. Winner will be randomly drawn on or about March 5, 1998 by Scholastic Inc., whose decisions are final. Potential winners will be notified by mail and potential winners and traveling companions will be required to sign and return an affidavit of eligibility. Prizes won by minors will be awarded to parent or legal guardian who must sign and return all required legal documents. By acceptance of their prize, winner and traveling companions consent to the use of their names, photographs, likeness, and personal information by Scholastic Inc., Parachute, Dualstar, and for publicity purposes without further compensation except where prohibited.

5. One (1) Grand Prize Winner will receive a trip for four to the set of Mary-Kate & Ashley's next production, located in Los Angeles, California. Trip consists of round-trip coach air transportation for four people from the major airport nearest winner's home to Los Angeles Airport; hotel accommodations for two (2) nights (two rooms or a quad room); and a visit to the set of the production to meet Mary-Kate and Ashley Olsen. Accommodations are room and tax only. Winner and traveling companions are responsible for all incidentals and all other charges, except the hotel tax, including but without limitations to meals, gratuities, all taxes and transfers. Dualstar, Parachute, and Scholastic Inc. reserve the right to substitute another prize if winner is unable to utilize prize within the time frame of the production schedule. (Total approximate retail value: $3,700.00)

6. Prize is non-transferable and cannot be sold or redeemed for cash. No cash substitute available. Any federal, state or local taxes are the responsibility of the winner.

7. Additional terms: By participating, entrants agree a) to the official rules and decisions of the judges which will be final in all respects; and b) to release, discharge and hold harmless Scholastic Inc., Parachute, Dualstar, and their affiliates, subsidiaries and advertising and promotion agencies from and against any and all liability or damages associated with acceptance, use or misuse of any prize received in this sweepstakes.

8. To obtain the name of the winner, please send your request and a self-addressed stamped envelope (excluding residents of Vermont and Washington) after March 5, 1998 to The Adventures of Mary-Kate & Ashley™ "Meet Your Favorite Stars" Sweepstakes Winners List, c/o Scholastic Trade Marketing Dept., P.O. Box 7500, Jefferson City, MO 65102-7500.

The party can't start without you...

Have You Read All Of Our Latest Adventures?

~The Adventures of~ MARY-KATE & ASHLEY™

Help Us Solve Any Crime By Dinner Time!™

☐ BBO86369-X *The Case Of The Sea World® Adventure™*
☐ BBO86370-3 *The Case Of The Mystery Cruise™*
☐ BBO86231-6 *The Case Of The Fun House Mystery™*
☐ BBO88008-1 *The Case Of The U.S. Space Camp® Mission™*
☐ BBO88009-8 *The Case Of The Christmas Caper™*
☐ BBO88010-1 *The Case Of The Shark Encounter™*
☐ BBO88013-6 *The Case Of The Hotel Who-Done-It™*
☐ BBO88014-4 *The Case Of The Volcano Mystery™*
☐ BBO88015-2 *The Case Of The U.S. Navy Adventure™*

$3.99 each!

It doesn't matter if you live around the corner...
or around the world...
If you are a fan of Mary-Kate and Ashley Olsen,
you should be a member of

MARY-KATE + ASHLEY'S FUN CLUB™

Here's what you get:
Our Funzine™
An autographed color photo
Two black & white individual photos
A full size color poster
An official **Fun Club**™ membership card
A **Fun Club**™ school folder
Two special **Fun Club**™ surprises
A holiday card
Fun Club™ collectibles catalog
Plus a **Fun Club**™ box to keep everything in

To join Mary-Kate + Ashley's Fun Club™, fill out the form
below and send it along with

U.S. Residents – $17.00
Canadian Residents – $22 U.S. Funds
International Residents – $27 U.S. Funds

MARY-KATE + ASHLEY'S FUN CLUB™
859 HOLLYWOOD WAY, SUITE 275
BURBANK, CA 91505

NAME:_____

ADDRESS:_____

CITY:_____ STATE:_____ ZIP:_____

PHONE: (____) _____BIRTHDATE:_____

The Adventures of MARY-KATE & ASHLEY™

Look for the best-selling detective home video episodes.

The Case Of The Volcano Mystery™ **NEW**		53336-3
The Case Of The United States Navy Adventure™ **NEW**		53337-3
The Case Of The Hotel Who•Done•It™		53328-3
The Case Of The Shark Encounter™		53320-3
The Case Of The U.S. Space Camp® Mission™		53321-3
The Case Of The Fun House Mystery™		53306-3
The Case Of The Christmas Caper™		53305-3
The Case Of The Sea World® Adventure™		53301-3
The Case Of The Mystery Cruise™		53302-3
The Case Of The Logical i Ranch™		53303-3
The Case Of Thorn Mansion™		53300-3

Join the fun!

You're Invited To Mary-Kate & Ashley's™ Sleepover Party™	53307-3
You're Invited To Mary-Kate & Ashley's™ Hawaiian Beach Party™	53329-3

And also available:

Mary-Kate and Ashley Olsen: Our First Video™	53304-3

DUALSTAR VIDEO

High-Falootin' Fun for the Whole Family!

OWN IT ON VIDEO!